Reach Into My Darkness
"I hate this place"

By
Lamont Carey

Edited by
Melanee Woodard
Valerie White
Libra Mayo

Book Design and graphics
Created by
Kia Kellibrew

Photo of Lamont Carey taken by
Rashidah Denton

Published by

ISBN: 978-0-9816200-2-2

Reach Into My Darkness-I hate this place

Special Thanks

Pharaoh, Melanee Woodard, Penny, Hermond Palmer, Jr., Felicia Bass, Dr. Adar Ayira, Robert Garrett, Brenda Richardson, Tyrone Hicks, Christine Graham, Rashidah Denton, Kevin Hicks, Valerie White, Afi, , Andrea Camille, Tom Brown, Wesui, Monday Childs, Alice Deal MS, and my social network family, my fans, and any and everyone I forgot.

Dear Student:

Guess what? You're different. It doesn't matter what race you are, what community you live in or what school you go to, you're different! And guess what else? People are going to try to group you together with other folks so they can assess you. That's for their own convenience. It doesn't have anything to do with who you are.

I want you to keep being you. There is nothing wrong with having an accent. There is nothing wrong with being from another country. There is nothing wrong with coming from your community. There is nothing wrong with being the smartest person in the class. There is nothing wrong with being the shortest or the tallest person you know. There is nothing wrong with being the lightest or darkest person in the building. There's nothing wrong with being the skinniest or thickest person in gym class. There is nothing wrong with YOU. Now something becomes wrong with you when you try to change who you are to fit it. You're never going to find happiness within yourself or others when you're pretending to be something you're not. If you do that, you lose you. You become fake. You're not keeping it 100! You know how ya like to keep it 100!

People are going to talk about you. Some are going to even get on your nerves but don't allow them to scare you into being someone or something you're not. You don't have to fight them to prove who you are. I know, I know, ignoring them doesn't always work. Sometimes folks just really don't know how to act. Sometimes you may have to confide in an adult to help you get the nerve wrecker away from you. Whatever you do, you do what you need to do to keep being who you are and working on the things you want to accomplish.

Let me tell you something else about people who are different! They have less drama because they are not caught up in the "he said", "she said", nonsense. People who follow the crowd usually end up in bad situations that they didn't start or they do crazy stuff to prove they are cool! Nonsense!

Also, don't mistake being "different" as being alone! Naaaaaaaw. That's not what I am writing. I am telling you that it is okay to be YOU. A lot of people who are different are the best dressers, best designers, smartest, coolest, confident and become the most successful.

For example, Do you think Bill Gates was a nerd in school? Now he is the richest man in the world! Do you think Oprah Winfrey was the coolest person in school? Now she is one of the richest and most popular people in the World! Do you think First Lady Michelle Obama was the best dressed girl in school? Now every woman wants to buy the outfit they see her in. All of these people were different. All of these individuals pursued something more important than fitting in. They focused on being the best person they could be and accomplishing their goals. That is true success and that is keeping it 100!

There is no failure in being true to yourself. There is failure in trying to be who you are not. Always and everyday continue to be uniquely you! You hear me Shawty.

FOREWORD

I was in school one day and looking at poems. There were so many different ones to choose from. But the internet is an awesome thing. I went to google, typed in a title (I Can't Read), and the first search was Lamont Carey on youtube. I watched it over and over. I was looking at the truth.

I became interested in Lamont Carey's work because he was talking about the life I was living. I wasn't doing so well in school and I wanted to count on my cheerleading, being an athlete, a dancer, drama or anything not related to school work to get by. And when I saw him reciting this poem about an 11 year old boy in the same grade as me, thinking just like me except he played basketball, and with a snap it was all over, I knew I wasn't alone but I knew I had to change.

I watched this poem so many times because I saw myself in it. I memorized it and practiced it alone and did it in a speech and poetry contest where I won 2nd place. I put on my acting skills and met Lamont Carey where I acted shy but it was one of the best things to happen to me.

Mr. Lamont Carey's work gives hope. Through his craft he teaches people that no matter what is going on good or bad that you can do great things. His work is something that we can all relate to at any age. If Lamont Carey could scribe a poem about a problem I had and I used it to change for the better, then I know that it can do the same for you. None of us are alone, we may think we are but his work helps us escape and realize the superstar inside of us.

As a young girl, I thank Mr. Carey for helping me believe

in myself. I believe that his work is real life issues of what us young children go through. He is a positive influence now and I am sure he will be for many more years to come.

Sierra Johnson
Age 12

TABLE OF CONTENTS

A Dude Like Me

See a dude like me.
I believe I am more inclined to fail than excel
So when I took pictures as a youngin I mimicked the dudes
in jail.

See a dude like me
I was told the quickest way to gold was through the streets
Because the white man ain't gonna let you eat.

See a dude like me
I was even told by women that a man ain't suppose to cry
So little punk dry your eyes.

See a dude like me
I grew cold and vicious and even took out witnesses.

See a dude like me.
I sat there eyes wide and ears open
As you narrowed my future with every word spoken.

See a dude like me
Was nothing but a kid that's how at twelve I ended up dead.

A dude like me.

I Was Born This Way

I fought me more than you do
Asking my reflection what's wrong with you
My joys and likes are all mixed
My parents and you want to fix it with your fists
I can't explain why I am not like you
Not loving the colors that you do
My choices don't match my private parts
But you hold it against my heart
I still fight me more than you do
Wanting to deny myself to stop angering you
It's wrong for me to love myself
I tried but I can't turn into this someone else
That I should be
Screaming in the mirror at stupid me
Girls should like Barbie and pink
Boys should like blue and football too
But my right mind must have been ditched
Or my body was switched
I fight me more than you do
Because you are allowed to just be you.

I Can't Read

I am eleven years old in the 6th. grade and I can't read
The class is so full that the teacher doesn't notice me
But I can't read
And when she finally asks me to come to the head of the
class
I do everything in my power to make the class laugh
What would u do if u knew that they all would laugh at u

But I can't read. I can't write. I can't spell and most of the
time
I don't know my left from my right

But they keep on passing me
Because I can dribble a ball
And I can hit a three pointer ya'll
And I can almost dunk
And I can guarantee u thirteen points

But I can't read. I can't write. I can't spell and most of the
time
I don't know my left from my right

And there are others in my class that I think are just like me
But they can't dribble a ball
And they can't dunk
So they can't guarantee ya' no points
So they are gonna have to work at McDonalds
But how they going to get a job when they can't read the
application
So the streets become their occupation

Now they are peddling drugs to our nation

But I can't read. I can't write. I can't spell and most of the time
I don't know my left from my right

And the teachers aide said that it is the teacher's fault
And the teachers blame the board of education
And the board of education says that it is my parents fault
And my parents blame me

But I can't read. I can't write. I can't spell and most of the time
I don't know my left from my right

On the biggest game of the school year I was coming down the lane
Getting ready to do my thang
When number thirteen crashed into me
And at the same time that I heard my knee crack
I saw my family's dream shatter
See they depended on me to get us out of the ghetto
So when I hit the ground I did everything in my power not to frown
But it was just too much pain
Like it ran straight to my brain
And the last thing I remember is the doctor saying
I will never run again
So now I am asking ya'll
What are my options
I can't read.

Kicking Cans

I used to kick beer cans on my way to school.
I never wanted to be the president.
I just wanted enough food to be filled.

I used to kick beer bottles on my way to school.
I never wanted to learn.
I just wanted better clothes to wear.

I used to cut through alleys on my way to school.
I never wanted justice.
I just wanted a television to watch.

I used to walk pass drug-dealers on my way to school.
I never wanted to be rich.
I just wanted to live better.

I used to speak to the drug-dealers on my way to school.
I never wanted to be a criminal.
I just needed some money.

What Love Does

He twisted her arm and blamed her for his pain
He cursed her and blamed her for his shame
He locked the doors in her brain
Until she found the nerve and ran
Declaring never again
Will a boy or a man
Turn his problems into her faults
Turning his fist into her jaw
That wasn't love she saw
He created war
When she wasn't the enemy
Love doesn't feel like captivity
It's the summer breeze
And when a hurricane comes you leave
She told me from under the scars under her left eye
The only way for a girl to survive
Is to love herself more than a guy
But it took time for her to decide
Her eyes had long ago went dry
Her fear became her determination
No longer trying to fix Satan
Because he won't change
Using his hands to bring her pain
Never again
And she said
Just so you know
Love glows
It's pure
It doesn't scare
Or threaten
Love needs no protection
No weapon

Love is a blessing
And if it doesn't feel that way
Love wouldn't make you stay
Where you're unhappy
That...love would never do
It wants what's best for you
Because love really does love itself some you.

Now My Plan Begins

Blessed with a gift I am told
Never understood if there was a connection to my soul
I always felt like a story that would never be told
I always wanted to be a voice
To inspire the mute that was their choice
So I let my actions speak louder than my words
I was told that is the only way to be heard
I was speaking the wrong tongue
Confused respect and fear with the use of an unauthorized
gun
See I was the darkness that was told I had a light
By an elderly woman that said you can try all you want but
The Creator is going to win the fight
I thought she was too religious
Associating The Creator and I… I thought she touched too
much of The Creator's liquor
She said The Creator didn't hang with saints
Sinners were the reason he came
She said you can't see The Creator because you are blinded
by material gain
I thought this woman was insane
In my eyes she saw the pain
She said that I would have to walk through fire before I
could understand The Creator's plan
She didn't understand
Hell was the afterlife that I expected
I remember her rubbing my face and saying by the grace of
The Creator you will be protected
I didn't respect that

If there was a Creator I was neglected
Deeper into the darkness
Quick to utter that I was heartless
Then I fell by the way side
And cried
Then I discovered a pen
I think if I had listened hard enough I would of heard my
Creator say, "Now my plan begins".

The "N" Word

They tell me that a house divided will never stand
So by me calling you the "N" word does that mean I
consider u three fifths of a man
Disrespecting you every chance that I get
And I don't know much about this dude name Willie Lynch
But I know I have never dated a sista with darker skin
And I use to hate it when light skinned dudes were in
And I say all this to state one fact
Don't call me the "N" word please don't call me that
Cause never could you use a word that was meant to
degrade me
and tell me it's a term of endearment
that's just like saying that slavery was one of our greatest
experiences
and I wish I could have shared it with my children
see that's insane
but quick to punch another race in the mouth if they call us
by that name
so why isn't it plain
that the word should be banned
I can hear Nate Turner turning over in his grave because he
is trying to understand
That he paved the way for this
And Martin had a dream and Malcolm threw up a fist
Just so we could call each other this
And I know we weren't suppose to read
So they give us the shortest month of the year to teach us
our history
But most of that was missing
It seems to begin with the rise of Martin

And after his assassination is when it ended
So I guess it is up to us to eradicate our own ignorance
So my first suggestion is…
DON'T CALL ME…
And STOP CALLING YOURSELVES…

NIGGAS.

Under The Street Light

We look just alike a lot would say
But I rarely look at you and you at me
We blame one another's generation
When we both are responsible for our lack of participation
I hate you
More for what you do
I don't know you on a personal level
And you're hating me because you were taught I sold my
soul to the devil
And when we are in the same room together
We don't speak to one another
But we talk behind the others back
You hating me for the influx of crack
And I hate you for selling it
I say because you're hurting our people
And your argument is I wasn't there for our young people
I keep my windows closed
Calling the cops when you begin to make noise
Fearful of all young black boys
Forgetting that I was once one
And that a little conversation can go along way son
But now I believe the newspaper…
 Young black boys are considered armed and dangerous
You consider me weak
Your justification because I pass you and I never speak
But what would I say
Your generation is responsible for the worse crimes of
today
I said that Dr. King would be pissed

And your reply would be that his generation stopped caring
So you hang under the street light
And I continue to think that whatever your doing out there
can't be right
But we never speak
And the sad part is that you look just like me
At least most would say
They just don't know that I am hating you and you're
hating me
And we never had a conversation
I'm judging you by the newspapers
And you're judging me for my lack of participation
In your life
One of these days, hopefully before I die, I will come and
stand with you under that street light.

You Showed Me

You were my strength
I watched you stumble through life on a daily basis
Your passion roared in your eyes so much that I
always looked away
You used words that my early education had not
taught me yet
You were my first teacher
You were my protector of the night
Your snoring let me know u were there
You reminded me that men don't always pee straight
Just come back and wipe off the toilet seat
U showed me that clothes don't define a man
So u wore what u chose
You taught me that singing off key
Doesn't mean u are not happy
U were so happy in limited space
U showed me what the future could be like for me
I give u much respect for that
You taught me that I should have wishes
U showed me life through your alcohol addiction.

Invisible Walls and Ceilings

I freed myself from my oppression

Locked inside of visible walls

Scars covering my body because I believed I
was destined to fall

So I fell...day in and day out

My mouth became as foul as the hallway that
leads to my door

My education crawled along my floor

I am poor

Poor beyond financial means

Mentally I am uneducated

I don't know too many people who have made
it

Not far beyond these invisible walls

I am told there is a ceiling

One that I could never touch

With these ceilings and walls life is too much

So I am limited and angry

Hating those that keep me locked in

And those that told me I am

I learn from the voices in my head

Not voices with no faces

But ones that lie in the staircase

Reminding me how the world is racist

And how slavery prevents my people from
making it

Long after emancipation

So I watch other flourish in this same nation

Looking at me saying that I am a waste

My people only congregate in church spaces

Outside you wouldn't know we were more than
just neighbors

Convinced that my life is only worth cheap
labor

So I am hating those that run across the boarder to steal my slavery

Now how am I suppose to feed my babies

Trapped behind this invisible wall and ceiling

Turning my anger into my own killing

The only way to express what I am really feeling

They say you back anything into a wall and it will become a villain

Invisible walls and ceilings

So education systems that make me believe that I am the victim

The one with the desk that will still pass me without teaching me

And the one that loves us enough to tell me I can't fly

There isn't no sky for me

Planting this in my brain before birth

Now I'm seeing in your eyes life ain't showed you nothing but hurt

Self-esteem gone because you never had self worth

But I am going to make this earth pay

I refuse to stay stuck behind these invisible walls just because ya' say

Because this world was meant for me!

So today these shackles are off,

These walls and ceilings are going to fall

I'm a tell the rest of the kids this is false

You can be anything you want

As long as you don't believe invisible ceilings and walls.

When kids play

The gun-shot woke up the whole house

She immediately shouts

Where are my babies!

He flings into a sitting position

Before running to where his gun was hidden

She bursts into her son's room

Her daughter stood over top of him with eyes
like the moon

He lie stiff from the corner of his mouth five
year old blood drips

Her lover stops in the doorway

First time the world knew that he could pray

She drops to her son's side

But she knew he was dead by his no longer blinking eyes

She cries

Her daughter whispers

I couldn't find start over to make him come alive

She looks up at the child barely thinking

But she sees the video game controller in one hand and the gun in the other

So who's to blame

the video game

Or his mother

Or the gun carrying lover.

Black Face

Some people tell me that I am pretty
I just don't see what they see
I wonder are they really seeing me
My skin is black
and the fact
 that I am black
how could they find beauty in that
So they lie to spare my feelings
Other folks I be hearing
The lighter you are
the further you are
from being all black
I am all of that
Dark-skinned
kinky split ends
and thick lips
TV only shows me to be Precious
A black girl scorn
worn
broken
Even I can't look in the mirror and focus
Ugly on the outside
 the inside hopeless
I must have been born and burned in sin
The only time I see a flicker of beauty is when I am
smiling
My teeth are white
My smile everyone likes

Until my mouth is closed
Monkey fo'sho.

Color of my parents

My mother is whiter than the coldest winter
My father is darker than the black hole
and I was born gold
with my mother's hair
my father's nose flair
My eyes are Caribbean blue
My lips are thin too
I'm beautiful
With my dad no one believes I'm his
with mom i must be an adoptive kid
I never fit in
I'm subject of debate any group I'm in
Stuck up and trying to be white
the darker color of my family recites
No where near being white
my mother parents ignite
Why do I have to choose to be black or white
Why can't I just be me
I am a mixture of the parents that gave birth to me
Or let me be red
The color of my parents love.

The Same Steps We Left

I stared across the table at him so perplexed
He looked over eyes completely vacant
Before dropping his elbows on his legs
Then lowering his head
I wasn't sure who I was madder at him or I
Feeling as if I really didn't try
Even though I know I gave my best
God, if this is a test
I don't know what I am doing
Looking at all of my past mistakes and all of the things I
have ruined
Although I changed my life
He only knows the beginning of all of the hype
He doesn't know all of the results
So how can I not feel at fault
I ran the streets
I fired the heat
At dudes that look just like me
Or even the police
Quick to scream that the world was against me
Embraced that fate
That if I die I am taking ya'll wit me
See the youngster don't care about the change
Invincible with the same thoughts that he was better at the
street game
Everybody is a loser
The victim and the shooter
Even the cops
And every community in the nation takes the shot
But the reason I feel ashamed

Because two more young black lives are ruined and I am to
blame
And I just learned their names
The deceased will never know mine
And the defendant I just watched him die
Before the judge handed down his sentence
He'll die in prison
I changed too late
Their father's and I should have been there to prevent this
fate
Our communities just can't wait
For us to play the game and then change
We are to blame
For our children being slain
They had direction
They followed the same steps we left them.

I Hate This Place

Eight years old I sat on the steps of my project building
With no shirt on or no shoes
Three steps beneath me sits John The Wino
He doesn't even know that I exist
But I can smell the liquor reeking from his flesh
That he has drunk for the last 35 years
And up walks Greg The Crackhead
And he stops three inches from me
And asked me
you got a dollar
I'm only eight
I don't have no money

I HATE THIS PLACE
And more than I hate the place
I hate the people
And more than I hate the people
I hate the looks in their eyes

Cause in their eyes I saw
No hope
In their eyes I saw no shame
In their eyes I did not see a dream
I did not see tomorrow
They were comfortable being who they were
Greg the crackhead and the wino
So I decided at eight that I'm going to do everything in my
power
To get the hell away from them
And the only thing that glows on my block is Pretty Ricky
See Pretty Ricky is the neighborhood drug dealer

And when I went to him
He let me in
You see drug dealers always need flunkies
So I held the guns
I held the drugs
And soon he let me sell
By nine I dressed fly
By the time I was 15 Pretty Ricky was in jail
So the block is mine
And I'm on my grind
And I will kill over a drug deal
But just like any block that's getting money
Other dudes be wanting your block
So three teens came up with a scheme
On how they can get my money
Gunshots echoed
Shot one three times
He didn't die on me
But as they tried me as an adult
He stood on the stand and testified against me
He did it
And he suppose to be a killa

I HATE THIS PLACE
And more than I hate the place
I hate the people
And more than I hate the people
I hate the looks in their eyes

And most would think I would be scared
Because I'm on my way to prison
But what they don't see
Is that this is a badge of honor for me

Because those that went before me
Told me glory stories
Like I had made out with female guards
I stabbed dudes
I still sold drugs
So this is a badge of honor for me
So I will return with stories

I HATE THIS PLACE
And more than I hate the place
I hate the people
And more than I hate the people
I hate the looks in their eyes

And when the bus rode into the prison
Before I had a chance to make any decision
The first person I see
Was Pretty Ricky
And he came to me
And said hide this
You're going to need that
He didn't tell me how to get me free
But instead he gave a knife to me
And this is my role model
The dude that I followed
Now we're back together again
As men
So he moved me into his dorm
And soon the drug game was back on
And then I started hearing stories that didn't seem right
Until late one night
Sherry that was born Tim
Walked into the bathroom

A few minutes later Pretty Ricky walked in behind him
Then I waited a few minutes or two
and I walked into the bathroom

I HATE THIS PLACE
And more than I hate the place
I hate the people
And more than I hate the people
I hate the looks in their eyes

So I stopped hanging with Pretty Ricky
Because this dude isn't the dude I thought him to be
So I did what they said that could get me free
I enrolled in school and got me a G.E.D.
Then three years later they set me free
Back on this block I hate

I HATE THIS PLACE
And more than I hate the place
I hate the people
And more than I hate the people
I hate the looks in their eyes

But now that I am free
I'm walking around with this G.E.D.
Because they told me
There would be many opportunities for me
But nobody would hire me
With felonies
So when I realized those were lies
So I fell back into my comfort zone
Back on this block that I used to own
Then a little kid that used to ride big wheels when I left

Approached me on the steps
And said O.G
This ain't the same neighborhood
That it used to be
No longer can you sell your drugs on these steps
So I said kid
Get out of my face before I peel your wigs
And as he walked away he just nodded his head
And as the sun started to go down
Before I could fully turn around
There was a tap on my back
And all I heard was one shot
But he shot me five times
Now I'm lying on the ground dying
I feel the wetness on my cheeks I must be crying

I HATE THIS PLACE
And more than I hate the place
I hate the people
And more than I hate the people
I hate the looks in their eyes

I hate the eyes of the young killer standing over top of me
with his glock
About to go down the path that I left
All over some steps

I hate this place
And more than I hate the place
I hate the fact that I died on the same steps
I tried to escape
I HATE THIS PLACE.

They'll Never Break Me

I remember walking down the hall in school
And kids use to pick on me like it's the coolest thing to
do
And I didn't know was it my shoes or my size
But I could see their hatred for me in their eyes
Even when they smiled
And sometimes I would say, "What did I do to make
you mad"
And some would ball up their fist
And say, "Get out of my face!
You really don't want to feel this"
So I would walk away
Still struggling to understand what did I do or say
To make them hate me
But I was determined...

They may shake me
But they'll Never Break Me

And my teachers don't understand
That if I tell, it wouldn't make them go away
It'll just give them a bigger reason to hate me
And I swear, I didn't do or say anything to make them
mad
But tell me what it is and I'll gladly take it away
Because I wanna take away
Their's and my pain
So I'll harbor the blame
So just tell me what it is and I'll make it go away
But it's me
Or my looks

Because they never gave me a chance to see if I was
cool
I guess because I didn't hang out with the cool kids
They considered me an outcast
Or somebody that's bad
But I'm really not all that innocent
Because I like to tell jokes
I also like to read
And my clothes...my parents just don't have the
money
So that's why I stay focused...
So I can get a degree
And one day get a job and make me some money
See...

They may shake me
But they'll never break me

And my mom and dad don't get it
They think if I just ignore them
They'll go away
But I've tried their suggestions but they don't work
And I'm tired of getting my feelings hurt
So sometimes I want to strike back
Because I can't change what it is they feel I lack
But I know
Violence doesn't get it
And I'm starting to see
That those kids are just like me
They trying to make friends so they pick on me
To hide their own insecurities
So they try to create some in me...

They may shake me
But they'll never break me

I've learned several ways to deal with bullies
And the first one is
To see if any of my friends
Are their friends
To see if they could get them to leave me alone
You know...Friends listen to friends
And the second one is
Talk to the bully when they're alone
But approach them with respect
And don't do it around their friends
Because peer pressure can turn it into a big old mess
And the third is
If you're being hit or hurt
You have to tell someone because your safety is at
risk
And keeping your mouth closed doesn't guarantee
The bully is going to unfold his fist
So safety comes first
Your life is the key
You can try all these ways
I suggested to deal with bullies
But remember...if you're being hurt
You got to tell someone
And you can never solve this problem with a gun
Remember...

They may shake me...
But they'll never break me.

Mommy's Little Man

My son is the man of the house

He's the only man I care about

He's the only man I need

Ain't that right, Baby

You don't want to be like your dad

You're my man

A man takes care of his home

Never leaves them alone

It's just you and I

Com'on, Little man, men don't cry

....So he doesn't

He's strong for her

He comforts her

He hides his frustrations

Impatiently waiting

To grow to a bigger size

Where opportunities lie

To become the man she really needs

At 9 he was offered a job in the streets

He took it to take care of mommy

You understand

He's her man

That's what he was told he is supposed to do

She knew the difference

But he didn't

He was just waiting for an opportunity to really fill his position.

I Hate Her

She stares at me with trembling fingers

And a half nervous jerk in the corner of her mouth that just lingers

Like she wants to cry

I want to feel compassion for her but I can't understand why

So I stare and watch her struggle

She starts off with "Baby Girl, you know I have always loved you."

I was just a young mother

Fighting back my overwhelming need to hug her

But she carried me through hell

Feeling like her saying she has always loved me makes my past better as well

At the same time my mind is screaming "I hate her"

But there is a whisper that says "She gave the best of her"

I'm trying to combat this forgiveness

But the hurt, pain, and abuse has been locked in my mental prison

Now I have the courage to let it out

But I can't bring myself to opening my mouth

And her pump hisses every time she breathes out her nose

So close to her Creator calling on her soul

My body begging to say I love and forgive u

But my tears are dry

from all those years I cried

to be loved so I don't know what to do

I guess my connection with her through the womb is making me crazy too

I have never felt like her baby

But I forgave her so many times in my life

The first half only because I couldn't move out to live my own life

Then when I became grown

I left her on her own

Felt she was finally free of me

So she should be happy

Now she calls me on her death bed

Trying to plead with me to forgive

Or lie to me at her bed side

I don't know what the fear is for I see in her eyes

Is it for me or because she is about to die

Why am I twisting and turning now

Should I get this off my chest and let her down

She wasn't there when I needed her

So I don't owe her any favors

So why has she waited to do this before death

I can only believe it is for her Creator she's trying to impress

She had all 40 years of my life to make this right

She never even called to see if this baby she says she loved was alright

And then tears leaked from the corners of her eyes

My mind screams "No" as I begin to cry

Before I hugged her

And told her I loved her

Then I sealed it with a kiss.

We all make mistakes but this is an opportunity that I just couldn't miss.

If she didn't teach me anything else, she taught me cruelty exist

And that I could never treat another person like this

And underneath my pain

My connection to her and my experience in life just taught me to understand

That everyone deserves another chance

Even if we don't believe they do

The only way to release our pain is give them the opportunity to release theirs too.

The War of Men

I feel like crying
Even when I am alone I look around to see if someone else
is spying
See a man is not suppose to cry
I never questioned why
I just don't do it
And most of the madness in my adult life I can barely make
it through it
But I have been conditioned
That a man only makes one kind of decision
Despite what he is feeling
He uses his mind to out think his heart
Ya' can understand why I am falling apart
Because my knees are carrying my tears
And I fear if I whimper the world would hear
And declare that I am weak
So I take the bumps and bruises but never speak
Have strength confused with stupidity
But still I remain ..:America's definition of a man
What I don't understand
I never met this author that put out the manual on how to be
a man
Most men believe in him
Most men die early because of him
And I too have taken this torch
And from a child held my tears back as I sat on this porch
Brain washing myself
Believing I could never use any help
Despite the pain of my inner self

Could never fully love a woman
Because never told I should listen to myself
Despite what I am feeling
I guess this is why it is easy for some men to walk away
from their children
So the average boy and man walks around broken
And feeling alone
Never feeling safe in the body that is home
I have been conditioned
Save your boys from going into the mental man's prison
Because by the age of four
He may start to believe that he is at war
With himself.

I Need A Gun

Gunshots let me know my peers are awake
My parents tell me paths on my street that I
should never take
Can't stay in the hallway
Or play out front
Neighborhood so afraid of guns
But everyone seems to have one
but me
or my family
My friends have died outside
Just because guns fired as they walked by
So I walk briskly through the streets
My mother says it would break her heart if it
happened to me
We live in fear
Like a soldier in a war where danger is always
near
But one of the ways to survive around here
is to show no fear
Because those that have guns don't run
Or hide inside
Or fear the hallway
So I pretend nothing frightens me
I just stay prepared to run
These are the reasons...
I need a gun.

She Weighed in Five Pounds Heavier Than Last Time

She weighed in five pounds heavier than last time

She tried her best to sigh

Her mind couldn't erase her tears

She didn't understand why she has been fighting weight gain for years

Food was her fear

And she didn't eat a lot

Her Metabolism held everything she got

Even her pain

And she was so ashamed

She tried all of the diets with the fancy names

her doctor told her that weight gain was in her genes

and if u asked her what she wanted to look like

she would reply anything that would hide the real her from her sight

then she met Ann

she weighed more than her but insecurities wasn't her friend

she held her head high

she only wore clothes that showed off her size

She walked with pride

and she could see the lust men had for Ann in their eyes

she asked Ann what was her secret

Ann told her the world finds fault in what u display as a
weakness

some are going to talk about you until their death that's just
people

and I never believed in anything such as everyone is equal

see I am unique

I don't have a twin so there will never be another that looks
just like me

see I am God's gift to this world

I am a big girl

but I am God's little girl

my size doesn't deprive me of anything I want

men, I get them by the bunch

clothes even if I have to order the ones I want

and fun I am always going to have

I had to grow into this because I didn't always laugh

I found peace in me

it would take more than my life time to tell the world why
they should love me

so I show them instead

but my focus is making sure I love me in my own head

u just have to find that place

learning to love that weight and that face

don't look to fit into society because u already do

and don't get caught up into the whispers because if u
change somebody is still going to talk about u

so just be u

no, be the u that u have been hiding

loving yourself is the cure to fighting a judgmental society.

Slave ship

Even if you hide it in a game
And it doesn't have action
Then the game loses it's attraction
Even if you put it in a rap with a smooth beat
And you don't show the consequences
Then your just adding to the false reality
And what you fail to realize is that people pay
attention
As long as somebody dies
So you have to show them the faces of all racists
And then they'll realize we all have hatred
See our society is built on violence
That's projected on another
Then you have them look into the eyes of one who
has killed his own brotha
Then they'll ask questions about how we got off track
Then you put'em on a slave ship to show when we
became black.

Learning To Be A Mommy

No more whispers
Now she screams before she hits her
Shaking her index finger at her Barbie
Just like mommy
I gave up my future for u
And I have to tell u more than once what to do
Not in my house
I will put your trifling self out
U have the nerve to poke your lips at me
I am the only one who loves you where is your daddy
Go pick that Barbie off the floor and get out my face
And don't even bother asking me for something to eat.

When Friends Become Enemies

Who will get stabbed in the back.

Someone shall feel cheated.

I look both ways for my cue.

A while ago it was neither of you.

Now I face a battle that I will lose.

I had nothing to gain but a lot at stake.

No two people are the same.

So three are definitely divided.

Who shall I go to .

I feel I should say something,

But two minds are hard to change.

Damn I hate these games.

I know I'll be blamed for something.

No one is mad at me…

Until two of my friends become enemies.

No Doubt

Trapped inside.

Inside a house of comfort...

Dreading the crack capsules that lie on my
welcoming mat.

To keep my child safe.

I must imprison him.

Play stations, MTV, CDs, and stereo systems I
scheme to keep him away from the curtains.

Behind it lies everything that can prevent him
from living.

It's too much excitement.

Laughing until gunshots echo.

They do.

Not a day goes by that one doesn't die holding
on to the designer clothes demands.

I can't go to work.

I'm afraid he'll open the door.

The outside will come in....

And steal my baby.

The White Page

Inhaling my imagination allows me to cover a white page with my vision.

       I love to write.

Undeveloped stories invade my mind and hold my dreams hostage.

       They force me to meet their demands.

These lead characters want to be respected, cherished, and most of all…
       They want to be living creations.

So for the past few years,

       I have been forced to give them life.

Now their dreams have become mine.

       I want the world to see these energetic,

       Persuasive,

       And lovable unknowns,

       Except,

By me.

I want to provide the masses with toasts given by my worlds.

This is the only way to regain my mind

FREEDOM.

Broken Dreams

You'll never succeed
You'll never achieve
All birds wings are broken
Staring in eyes that are hopeless
So they spew
an unfair society on you
Where your dreams are liars
How the world is deniers
How they tried to fly
Toward the false skies
So they swat your dreams
To protect your wings
From being broken
A few setbacks made them hopeless
When they should have refocused
Used those mistakes as steps
To analyze on how to overcome the next
But instead sat
moped
Abandoned all hope
Their own mistakes
Some you'll make
Don't let their words block you
stop you
From believing
You're not them
Those who achieve
Never stop trying
Or believing
It's not doable
Your dreams belong to you
As long as you don't stop...
Trying to fly.

Ineffective As A Dad

I love you
This isn't an excuse
Or me trying to justify
but I love you
From the moment I looked into your eyes
I feel in love with you
Wanted to protect you
Provide for you
Put you in a house that my pockets say that I could
never own
See most nights I didn't even make enough money to
bring you pampers home
And if your mother wasn't feeding you from her chest
You probably would have starved to death
But your smile is my pride
And the reason I stay so torn up inside
Because a father's number one responsibility is to
provide
And that I couldn't do for you
And if it wasn't for the baby shower that your mother
threw
For you
On your birth, I would have only had one outfit for you

So this made me feel
Ineffective as a dad
And less than a man
So I figured without me your life would have a better
chance
So I left

This had nothing to do with whether I loved you

I have always loved you
It just became to unbearable to look at you
And I tried to get a good job for so long
I even done some wrong
Just so you could have birthday presents to unwrap
But I was constantly tormented by the times we would
walk in a store
And you would grab a candy bar for your daddy to
purchase
And I would say no
And go as far as to lie to you
To say no candy is good for kids
But the truth is
I couldn't afford something for under a dollar for my
kid
So this made me feel
Ineffective as a dad
And less than a man
So I figured without me your life would have a better
chance
So I left

How am I suppose to lead a kid that I can't even feed
How am I suppose to teach a kid at the age of three
Who shows more intelligence than me
I just knew sooner than later you would see the
ineffectiveness of your daddy
And I know, you don't care about those things
You want to spend time with your dad
You want to be loved by your dad
But I thought, my presence wasn't enough
That my love wasn't enough
Because you need things
and I couldn't afford your basic necessities

So this made me feel
Ineffective as a dad
And less than a man
So I figured without me your life would have a better
chance
So I left

And when my financial situation improved
I wanted to run to you
Provide for you
Do all the things that a father is supposed to do
But I knew
so much time had passed
that you would reject me as your dad
And I didn't want to deal with that shame
Didn't want to take us through that pain
So I stayed away
Now I know every decision that I made was a mistake
And I became ineffective as a dad the minute I
allowed my fears
to make me... go away.

Treasures

In everyone's life ..
There is something one treasures more than life itself.
This precious treasure has to be glorified…
As a gift from The Creator.
Even my inner most feelings could never express the joy
that my thoughts have captured and stored away inside my
heart.
My eyes have not seen no other.
My eyes will never mistaken…
Your voice.
Darkness could never make you a memory.
You mean to me what no other has meant.
You are what no other could be.
You are….

My mother.

When Murder Happens

When violent cartoons
Turn into kids on the news
When grassroots organizations
Preach hatred
When politicians
Forgets the nations best interest
When fairytales become better than life
When man and woman come together without being
husband and wife
Who pays the price for our rights and wrongs
When innocent eyes find it hard to understand right from
wrong
When daddy's gone and mommy's asleep
Whose feeding the babies?
We say the music
We say the TV.
These are only distractions to escape our responsibilities
So who's to blame?
When children misbehave
When teachers feel the need to carry guns
When mothers kill sons
When preachers kill children
When looking for love kills children
When dreams kill children
When children kill children
When religion kills children
When poets kill children
When fear kills children
When hopelessness kills children
When you kill children

When I kill children
When are we going to remember our children?
When they're dead
On the news
Then we will remember they were in our care
Your children
My children
Are our children
Reach the children
Before they become dead children.

Run Kim Run

Kim was scared
A young girl harboring such fear
When Rick screamed at her in the streets
None of Kim's friends even tried to speak
On her behalf
A few of Rick's buddies stood there and laughed
One tried to break it up
By whispering, com'on man, that's enough
Rick looked at him with evil eyes
Then his friend stood there with his school
books at his side
Rick scanned the streets
Too many people somebody will probably call
the police
So he smiled at her and told her to go home
alone
With her book bag
She walked away from her friends

Run Kim. Run

The next day
Rick caught Kim walking down the school
hallway
He asked her, do you still love me
She nodded her head that she did
He said at lunch period lets go get something to
eat
As they walked down the street

a male student spoke to Kim
But she knew better than to speak back to him
Rick still plucked her on the side of her head and
asked who was he
She said, nobody
Rick stopped and looked her in her eyes
If I find out you lie
you die

Run Kim. Run

Kim started to stay up most of the night
Writing in her journal how Rick has completely
changed her life
Isolated her from her friends
Constantly threatening he'll kill her parents
If she ever told
Betta make sure her friends keep their mouths
closed
She felt so alone
Then her phone would ring
he would immediately scream
You must be talking to another guy
Cause you up late
Don't even lie
Look out the window...I'm outside

RUN KIM. Run

The next day at school she saw Rick at the end
of the hall
Playing with a tennis ball
he told her to come to him

As she passed the principal's office she decided
to go see him instead
She told the principal about the hits
and the shouts
and about the time he bloodied her mouth
She let it all out
and felt so free
the first thing the principal did was call the
police
Rick didn't even know to run
He was still waiting for her to come
But the police came
and asked him his name
He said Rick
They immediately arrested him for domestic
violence
And if you would ask Kim today
What she would say
If your boyfriend or girlfriend was treating you
this way

Run Kim! Run!
But tell someone who can help
Domestic violence isn't an issue you can stop by
yourself.

Confidence

Somebody told me that my creator says nobody's perfect
So when I get up in the morning and I look into the mirror
I immediately notice my imperfections
Like I don't smile a lot
Because I know I have gaps in between my teeth
And the only reason that this matters to me
Is because I Lack Confidence
And when I get dressed I tend to dress in front of that full
mirror
And try to decide if this is an outfit that you would like to
see me in
And the only reason that this matters to me
Is because I Lack Confidence
Or when I go to the barbershop
I tend to get the haircut that I think that you would like
And the only reason that this matters to me
Is because I Lack Confidence
And when I eat in public
I tend to eat very small amounts
Because I am afraid that my weight will get out of hand
That you would snicker and talk about me behind my back
And the only reason that this matters to me
Is because I Lack Confidence
Or when I step up on the scale
And the scale reads 130 pounds
I immediately think that you think that I am anorexic
And the only reason that this matters to me
Is because I Lack Confidence
Or when I am walking down the street
She's so fine and that's a woman that I would like to meet

But I don't open my mouth to say a word
But when she passed me
She smiled at me
So she might have even liked me
And the only reason that this matters to me
Is because I Lack Confidence
Or when I go to the car lot
I pick a car that my friend would want to drive
This is my ride
But I have already placed myself on the passenger side
And the only reason that this matters to me
Is because I Lack Confidence
So through my trials and tribulations
I seem to can't make it
So I fall
And I fall
And I keep on falling
And I keep on falling
And when I tried to pull myself up
I'm not doing it for me
I am still trying to perfect who I think that ya'll want me to
be
So I keep on falling
And I keep on falling
And I keep on falling
Until I finally hit the bottom
And I HAVE JUST HAD ENOUGH
So when I got out of bed this morning
I put on the clothes that I wanted to wear
And I smiled at myself in that full mirror
And said
When I walk out this door
You don't have to like me

Want me
Need me
You don't even have to speak to me
But I ain't going nowhere
So you better prepare
Because I NO LONGER LACK CONFIDENCE!

Stop & Frisk

They suspect me

No desire to protect me

Just arrest me

Like my skin is a mask

Slowly begin to drive pass

Then they stop

The cops

They search me like terrorists

My emotions I bury quick

Any outburst

Can get me hurt

But my internal pain

My internal shame

Makes me want to scream

But I don't

I won't

Learning to take the humiliation

My only goal is to get to a safe location

And not the police station

Or the morgue

I used to think they were bored

This is where they suppose to be

Harassing me

And they wonder why I don't speak

Or no one in my neighborhood talks to the police

They don't come to protect me

Just to catch me.

Testing The New Dude

I know this unwritten rule
New neighborhoods or schools
Every location
I have to set the expectations
Erase any doubts where my heart lies
Look dudes in their eyes
Body language telling them don't even try
I ain't broken or weak
I'ma walk your streets
It's better we get along
Or something will really go wrong
Cause I ain't scared
Been through this so many times and I ain't dead
My momma moved us here
So I ain't going nowhere
Until we have to move again
This is the way I either make a new friend
Or crush a new enemy in his den
So his friends will know
Don't mess with the new dude
I go through this every time we move
Feeling pressure to prove
That I got heart
So now the fights I start
To get it over with
The initiation with the dudes I never asked to hang
with.
What I don't understand
Why do I have to always prove I am a man
With my hands
To gain respect
Manhood doesn't seem to be defined by my intellect
That seems to be a weakness or makes me soft

And the adults say it's all my fault
Like they don't know this unwritten rule
That you have to test the new dude.

The Monster

Really look at me
You judge me from what you can't possibly see
Discriminate against me
Label me
And watch me closely
You scare me

Your mouth never opens to me
But you would declare that you know me
Overwhelming need to control me
You write horror stories
How I steal your glory
But you ignore me
When I speak
You would declare I am the freak
You scare me

Define me by my clothes
Define me by things you can't possibly know...
About me
What I eat
How I think
What I drink
Where I go
You created a me that I don't even know
You scare me

You want everyone to be aware of me
To not trust me
To not comfort me
But to discuss my flaws
How my life will evolve
and whither away
When you don't even know

You scare me

But you declare your scared of me.

LATE NIGHT

Tonight leaks with a calm that terrorizes my peace
Solitude is the biggest threat to my security
Sitting on a fence that has given way to the struggle
It is hard to watch the moon entertain a sky full of
stars
When the street light keeps blinking
Shadows moving in the dark with no body parts
So it must be the trees.
And tonight they don't even breathe because it's so
calm
But my ears are so alarmed
They keep my eyes unfocused
And the heart beats so fast that my palms keep
moving
And the teddy bears tied to the tree
remind me of a voice that's missing
Of the block that's missing
Of a race that's missing
But I am sure most of the voices are in prison.

What Love Is

She declared
that all young girls should know
That a boy who loves you
Will never try to isolate you
Control you
And that your beauty isn't the cause of his insecurities
Those are his imperfections to fix
And love doesn't scream
Love isn't mean
Love is uplifting
Protecting
and nurturing
A boy's hands are his own
And should never be hurting you
His hands should take away your pain
Catch you when you're falling
Support you when your climbing
And his words
Should be used to empower you
To compose poetry for you
They should never be used against you
Because love
Doesn't hurt
Love doesn't have holes
And he can never make you whole
A boy who wants to be a good man
Should understand
That you are beautiful
That he is beautiful
And neither of you lose yourselves together
Because love builds
It never destroys
And when you see each other be filled with joy
And not fear

Because love doesn't scare
It declares
That I love having you here.

A MESSAGE TO MY SON

There will come a time
When girls will consume your mind
You'll be so infatuated
You'll linger on every word of their conversations
It's true...
Girls are amazing too
But you must understand
As a respectable young man
That there are rules you should always respect
In your relationships
That she will never be
Your property
You have no control
Over what she does or where she goes
And when she says, no...
She means, no
And if she cares for you
She will be faithful to you
And you to her
That is part of respecting and loving her
And communication means you have to participate in
conversations
And not just listen
Because you both have to be active in making your
relationship decisions
And relationships have their disagreements
Don't be too quick on leaving
And a man's hands
Should never be used to strike a woman
And her hands should never be used
To hit you
Fighting isn't loving
Controlling isn't loving

You show love by treating her like she wants to be
treated
She wants to feel needed
Never beaten
And if you can't get along
It's okay for the both of you to move on
Because every relationship doesn't necessarily work
And neither of you should remain
if you are physically
Mentally
or emotionally hurt
Respecting each other must come first
I know you understand
Because I raised you to be a decent
and proud young man.

THE HATER BEFORE ME

The haters before me

are easier to c

I cast them away from me

Then left alone

Split in half now two personalities living within the body I call home

One doubts my success

Makes the other restless

How do u fight

The hater that u gave the breath of life

The war between self is harder to win

I welcome the outside haters but fear the ones within

I find it hard to breathe

Springs forth my creativity

With no direction

Words people find breathless

I find escape

Words empower and terrorize me

Standing on the edge

Considering jumping from the ledge

So I close my eyes

And spring forth

wings appear and I fly

The beauty inside me

Is only the creativity

What makes up the rest of me

Lamont breathe

THE END

I hope none of these poems were a reflection of your life. However, I do hope that you were able to somehow identify and connect with some of the issues addressed. It would be really cool if one of these poems inspired you to talk about something that you may be going through or have experienced. If nothing else, I hope you learned that we all have traumatic events in our lives.

These events are situations some of us may have to find our way out of. Those situations don't define who we are but they can show us how mentally, physically and spiritually strong we are.

The greatest lesson I have learned is that I am amazing. I had to overcome so many bad situations to find out what I wanted to do with the rest of my life. I discovered that I was unique but my bad experiences weren't so unique. Thousands of people have gone through similar situations but didn't survive. Me, I not only survived but I found my voice. I found my passion. I write. Writing helps me release the ugliness I see in this world. Writing helps me share my opinion. Writing helps me to teach others how to locate their voice and to free that voice.

I hope you realize that you are not only unique but you are also amazing. Everything you could ever want to be and accomplish in your life you can. Anything and everything is possible. There are no limitations in your life if you put your mind to it and follow through with determination and actions. You just have to be brave enough to live your life unafraid to be YOU.

Now I want to THANK YOU for taking the time to read this book. Here are some other projects I have released:

IMAGINE CD

Lamont Carey's award winning CD containing such hits as "I Can't Read", "Confidence", "I Hate This Place", "She Says She Loves Me", and ten other electrifying spokenword pieces.

Learning To Be A Mommy-The Play (DVD)

Lamont Carey's second play directed at the John F. Kennedy Center. A story about a young girl who struggles while making sure her family is safe, healthy, and protected. She has to make some choices that could leave her dead and her family destroyed.

Upcoming projects of mine:

The Business Side Of Spokenword

This book is a blueprint on to how to maximize your money making potential as an artist. It covers everything from protecting your material to securing performance opportunities.

Visit my personal website: www.lamontcarey.com or my Youtube Channel at www.youtube.com/ lamontcarey1. You will find exciting videos of some of my performances, film projects, speaking engagements, my stage-plays and others performing my work from around the world.

Booking Lamont:

Lamont Carey is not only an author, he is an international award-winning spokenword artist, filmmaker, playwright and motivational speaker.

To arrange to have Lamont Carey speak or perform at your next event anywhere in the world, contact LaCarey Management at:
lacareyentertainment@yahoo.com

You may visit the website at:
www.lacareyentertainment.com
www.lamontcarey.com
FB: LaCarey Entertainment, LLC
Twitter: @lamontcarey

Send fan mail to:

LaCarey Entertainment, LLC
P.O. Box 64256
Washington, DC 20029

CPSIA information can be obtained
at www.ICGtesting.com
Printed in the USA
FFOW04n1529180715
15183FF